Gulliver Taschenbuch 76

Janosch, geboren in Zaborze, Oberschlesien, arbeitete in verschiedenen Berufen, ab 1953 als freier Künstler. Er lebt heute auf einer einsamen Insel. Er veröffentlichte zahlreiche Kinder- und Bilderbücher sowie Romane, zum größten Teil im Programm Beltz & Gelberg. Für *Oh, wie schön ist Panama* erhielt er den Deutschen Jugendbuchpreis.

A Letter for Tiger

Translated by Anthea Bell

BELTZ
& Gelberg

Gulliver Taschenbuch 76
© 1980, 1982, 1990 Beltz Verlag, Weinheim und Basel
Programm Beltz & Gelberg, Weinheim. Alle Rechte vorbehalten
Ausgabe in englischer Sprache
für die Bundesrepublik Deutschland, Österreich und die Schweiz
© der englischen Übersetzung bei Andersen Press Ltd., London
Reihenlayout und Einband von Wolfgang Rudelius, Einbandbild von Janosch
Gesamtherstellung Druckhaus Beltz, 69494 Hemsbach
Printed in Germany
ISBN 3 407 78076 1
7 8   97

One day, when Little Bear was setting
off to go fishing in the river again, Little
Tiger said:

»Bear, I feel so lonely when you're away. I wish you'd write a letter home, to cheer me up. Please do!«

»All right,« said Little Bear, and he took a bottle of blue ink with him. He also took a canary's feather, because you can write very well with a canary quill pen.

He took some notepaper too, and an envelope for his letter.

When he was down by the riverside, first he put a worm on his hook, and then he put the hook and line in the water, and then he picked up the quill pen and wrote a letter on the notepaper, in blue ink. It said:

»Dear Tiger,
This is to let you know that I am very
well. How are you? Please peel the onions
and boil the potatoes while I'm out.

I may bring home a fish for supper. With
love and kisses from Little Bear.«
Then he put the letter in the envelope
and stuck it up. He caught two fish: one
to eat, and one to be put back in the
water to cheer it up, because everyone
likes to feel cheerful.
When evening came he picked up his
fish and his bucket, his ink and his quill
pen, and the letter too, and he started for
home.
Wait a minute, Little Bear! You nearly
forgot your fishing rod!

»Oh yes, so I did! Thank you very much,«
says Little Bear.
When he reached the top of the hill, he
began calling out:
»A letter! For Tiger!
A letter! For Tiger!«

But Little Tiger did not hear him. Tiger was lying in the grass behind their little house.

He had not peeled any onions or boiled any potatoes. He had not swept the living room floor or watered the flowers. He had not wanted to do anything at all, because he still felt so lonely.

And now he did not even want his letter,
either.

Because Little Bear was home again
himself, in person.
That night Little Tiger woke Little Bear
up. »Listen, I must just ask you something before you go to sleep,« he said.
»Could you send your letter rather earlier
tomorrow? Perhaps you could send it by
express messenger.«
»All right,« said Little Bear, and next day
he took all his things out with him
again. The ink, the quill pen, notepaper,
and an envelope.

But today he took a stamp too.

Down by the riverside, he put the worm
on the hook and he put the hook and
line in the water again.
Then he wrote:
»Dear Tiger,
Please do all the things I asked you to
do when I wrote yesterday. I hope you
are well. In haste! With lots of love and
kisses from Little Bear.«
Then the elegant goose came by.

»Could you deliver my letter, please? It's for my friend Tiger, at home.«

»So sorry,« said the elegant goose. »I'm in a dreadful hurry. I have to attend a funeral.«

Then the fat fish came by.
»Could you deliver my letter, please? It's
for –« But the fish had shot off again
already.
Fishes are quick movers.
And perhaps hard of hearing, too.

Then the mouse came running by, very
light on her feet.
Yes, she said, she would deliver the letter.
But along came a little blue wind. It filled
out the letter like a sail, and it almost
blew letter and mouse and all away.

Then the fox came by.
»Could you deliver my letter, please,
Mr Fox?« asked Little Bear. »It's for my
friend Tiger, at home.«

»Your friend Tiger, at home?« said the fox. »So sorry, I can't spare the time. I have to attend the elegant goose's funeral with her.«

Life is short, little goose!
Then the elephant came by, in his boat.

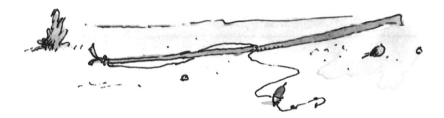

»Hi! Elephant!« shouted Little Bear.
»Come here! Listen!«
But the elephant must have been asleep,
because he did not move.

The donkey with the rucksack on his back would not deliver the letter either. Nor would the little man with the long nose.

But then the hare came by, wearing his
fast running shoes.
»Mr Bear, give me your letter!
It will get there all the better.
Stamp it, then your job is done.«
Now run, hare, run, hare, run!
And the hare ran as fast as the wind, as
fast as lightning, as fast as his shoes
would carry him. He ran to Little Tiger,
at home.

Little Tiger had not felt like doing anything that day either. He had not peeled
any onions or boiled any potatoes. He
had not swept the living room floor. He
had not even lit the stove.

»A letter for Tiger!« cried the fast hare,
and Little Tiger jumped up and shouted,
»Where, why, what, when? Who's it for
and who's it from?«

»It's for Tiger,« said the hare.

»Oh well, I'm Tiger myself, so hand it
over!«

Tiger danced for joy. He danced on the
table, he danced on the chair, he danced
on the bed and he danced on the sofa.
He read the letter from beginning to end,
and then he read it from end to beginning.

He felt like doing all sorts of things now.
He peeled the onions and boiled the potatoes. He swept the floor. Life was good.
He lit a nice hot fire in the stove, and
picked parsley in the garden to go with
the delicious fish they would have for
supper.

And when Little Bear came home, they spent a cosy evening together. They had fish and hot potatoes for supper, and they drank spring water from the well. After their nice supper, they had a lovely time dancing and singing and playing music. One of the two friends played the wooden-spoon-fiddle, and Tiger played the broomstick-double-bass.
Far away, the happy mole heard the beautiful music, and he came to visit them at once.

He danced a romantic waltz with his walking stick, on the table.

»This is the happiest day of my whole life,« said Little Tiger. And that was no lie.

That night, Little Tiger woke Little Bear up. »There's something I just wanted to tell you before you go to sleep,« he said. »*You* can get the letter tomorrow, to cheer you up too! A letter for me one day, and a letter for you the next. Good night!« Next day, Little Tiger took his basket for gathering mushrooms, and the bottle of blue ink and the canary quill and the notepaper, and he went out into the wood.

It was his turn to write Little Bear a
letter today. He wrote:
»Dear Friend Little Bear,
I am writing you a letter so as to cheer
you up. I hope we shall meet again soon.
This evening there will be mushrooms
for supper...

…mushrooms stewed in butter. I can see them growing close to me here. With love and kisses from your affectionate friend Tiger. P.S. Wait for me.«

And so it went on, day after day. One day Little Bear wrote to Little Tiger, and the next day Little Tiger wrote to Little Bear. The fast hare was their postman.

One night, Little Tiger woke Little Bear up.

»Listen,« he said, »why don't we write Auntie Goose a letter some day? That would cheer her up, too. All right?«

So they wrote their Auntie Goose a letter the very next day. They sent her lots of love and kisses, and hoped she was well, and so on.

Then Auntie Goose wrote to her Cousin
Hedgehog.
And Cousin Hedgehog wrote to the little
man with the long nose.

The elephant wanted to write to his wife
in Africa.

»I can't go all the way to Africa,« said the
fast hare. »That's air mail. The carrier
pigeon takes air mail letters.«

Now that everyone was writing letters, the fast hare could not deliver them all by himself. He asked the other hares who lived in the wood to come and be post-men too.

»You must be very fast, and very discreet,« he said. »You mustn't read the letters, and you mustn't tell anyone what's in them, understand?«

»We understand,« said the hares in their fast running shoes, and sure enough, they all understood.

Boxes were hung on all the trees, to take the letters, so that the hares would not have to call on everyone to fetch them. The boxes were painted yellow.

One day Little Tiger said, »You know, Little Bear, when you're in the living room and I'm in the kitchen, I still feel lonely.«

So they got the garden hose and laid it between the two rooms. Now they had a telephone in their house.

»Can you hear me? Hullo, hullo! Can you hear me? Who is it speaking?«

»It's Mr Bear speaking, and I can hear you loud and clear.«
»You know what?« said Little Tiger. »We could lay a telephone line in the river too. Then I wouldn't have to work so hard at writing letters the whole time.«
So that was what they did.
They laid an underwater cable.

»Suppose we had a telephone line like that under the ground?« said Little Tiger. »Then we could ring up Auntie Goose on the other side of the wood.«
So the moles dug them an underground telephone system. The lines went from here to there and from hither to thither, in fact all over the place.
»Hullo, Auntie Goose, this is Little Tiger. Can you hear me, Auntie Goose? Yes, it's me! Lit-tle Ti-ger! The one with the little stripy tail behind him. Your nephew!«
»And this is Little Bear,« said Little Bear. »Tell her I'm here too, Tiger!«

The elephant phoned the telephone exchange.

»Operator speaking! Operator speaking! Africa? No, I'm sorry, we have no lines to Africa. Goodbye.«

»Oh well,« said the elephant, »never mind. I'll write an air mail letter instead.«

And now everyone who lived in the wood or by the riverside could write letters to everyone else, and you could ring up your girl friend long distance if you liked. Wasn't that wonderful?

»Oh, Bear,« said Little Tiger. »I do think life is tremendously good, don't you?«

»Yes,« said Little Bear. »Tremendous and good.«

And if you ask me, they were quite right.